W9-DBG-976

DISNEY Tangled The Series

TALES OF RAPUNZEL 1

Secrets Unlocked

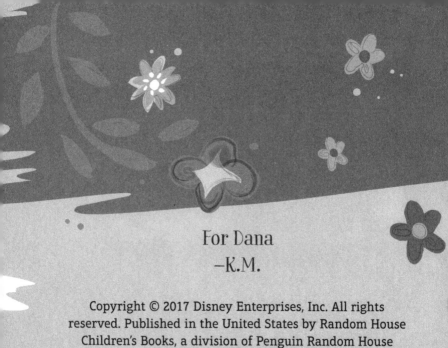

For Dana
—K.M.

randomhousekids.com

ISBN 978-0-7364-3826-1 (trade) —
ISBN 978-0-7364-3827-8 (lib. bdg.)

Printed in the United States of America

10 9 8 7 6 5 4 3 2 1

Random House Children's Books supports the First Amendment and celebrates the right to read.

Disney
Tangled
The Series

TALES OF RAPUNZEL 1

Secrets
Unlocked

Adapted by
Kathy McCullough

Illustrated by
the Disney Storybook Art Team

Random House New York

Long ago, in a kingdom called Corona, there lived a king and queen who eagerly awaited the birth of their first child. When the queen fell ill, the king ordered his guards to search for a cure. Finally, one was found: a golden flower that had grown from a single drop of sun. After drinking a broth made from the flower, the queen recovered and gave birth to a beautiful baby girl with hair the color of the sun. The king and queen named their daughter Rapunzel.

The kingdom rejoiced at Rapunzel's arrival—but before the baby was even a year old, she was taken. Her captor, an old crone named Mother Gothel, knew the flower's healing magic had been reborn in Rapunzel's blond hair. Part of its power was the ability to make someone eternally young. Mother Gothel wanted the magic all for herself.

Mother Gothel locked Rapunzel in a tower deep in the woods on the outskirts of Corona. The princess spent the next eighteen years there with only her pet chameleon, Pascal, for company. Then, one day, with the help of a thief named Flynn Rider, she escaped. Flynn cut Rapunzel's hair, destroying its power, and Mother Gothel instantly turned to dust. Rapunzel and Flynn—whose real name was Eugene Fitzherbert—fell in love, and Rapunzel was finally reunited with her parents.

Rapunzel's hair, now short and brown, had lost its magic, but she no longer needed it. She was home safe, surrounded by loved ones, with a world of new experiences to explore. It seemed certain she would live happily ever after . . .

But as each new day brought new adventures, there was also the possibility of new dangers . . . and new mysteries.

On one such day, Rapunzel and Cassandra, Rapunzel's friend and lady-in-waiting, decided to venture beyond the walls of the kingdom to visit the spot where the magic golden flower had been found. A stone marker had been placed where the flower had grown, at the edge of a high cliff.

They arrived at twilight, and Rapunzel was

surprised to see spiky black rocks jutting up through the ground around the marker.

"They sprouted up about a year ago," Cassandra told her.

Curious, Rapunzel reached out toward one of the rocks. There was a sudden explosion of bright light, and new rocks burst up from the earth.

Rapunzel and Cassandra fled, but the rocks pursued them. More and more rocks appeared, each one larger and more threatening than the last.

As Rapunzel ran, her hair grew long again—as long as it had been before she left the tower. It also changed from its tawny brown to a golden yellow, the color of the sun.

Rapunzel didn't have time to react—she had to escape from the rocks. She and Cassandra ran as fast as they could, racing across the stone bridge that led back to the kingdom. Although the rocks tried to follow them, the bridge crumbled, and the vicious rocks were left behind.

But Rapunzel remained haunted by the memory of the sinister rocks, and by the many questions her encounter with them had raised. . . .

Rapunzel's bare feet slapped against the marble floor as she chased Pascal down the wide hall of the castle. Her long blond hair, tied up in a braid, flew out behind her.

Pascal tried to blend in with one of the statues along the wall. His skin turned from green to gray to match the stone of the statue, but Rapunzel spotted him and he ran off.

Rapunzel and Pascal used to play hide-and-seek in the tower, but there hadn't been many places for either of them to hide. Now that they lived in a castle, there were endless places to hide.

9

There were dozens of halls and hundreds of rooms. There were passageways and tunnels. There were so many places to explore, Rapunzel still hadn't discovered them all.

Pascal slipped around a corner. Rapunzel followed him and spotted King Frederic and Queen Arianna talking to Eugene. Rapunzel paused to hug her parents and give Eugene a quick kiss on the cheek before hurrying off after Pascal, who had darted into a room at the end of the hall.

Rapunzel entered the room and noticed a cloaked figure standing at the far window. She felt a sudden chill.

The figure turned and lowered her hood. It was Mother Gothel! Her curly black hair seemed electrified. When she raised her arms, spiky black rocks suddenly sprouted in front of *her. The rocks tore up the floor, as if they were marching toward Rapunzel.*

As the rocks got closer, Rapunzel's blond hair began to glow. Blinding light crackled between her hair and the rocks, causing her hair to come loose from its braid and fly around her in a shimmering golden swirl.

"Your hair has returned!" Mother Gothel cooed in her silky voice. "Isn't it wonderful? Come now, dear. It's time to get you back to the tower, where you'll be safe." The rocks thundered closer.

Rapunzel was frozen in terror. She couldn't move. She couldn't speak. Everything went black as she heard Mother Gothel shriek, "Rapunzel!"

Rapunzel's eyes snapped open and she jerked up in bed. Her blond hair flew up around her. She took a deep breath, calming herself, as her hair floated back down onto her shoulders like a protective blanket.

It was only a dream. She was in her room in the castle, safe and sound. Mother Gothel was dead and gone.

But the rocks . . . They were a new threat. Rapunzel once again recalled the night she had first seen them, and how they had caused her short brown hair to grow long and blond again. She shivered, remembering how the rocks had chased her and Cassandra down from the cliff.

The rocks hadn't followed them to the castle, though. So why had they appeared in her dream?

It seemed to Rapunzel that the dream was a warning.

But *what* was it trying to warn her *about*?

"The dreams are trying to tell me something, Cass," Rapunzel told Cassandra later that morning. They were in Rapunzel's bedroom, where Cassandra was braiding Rapunzel's hair. Pascal sat on a pillow on Rapunzel's nightstand and watched.

"Why were those rocks on the cliff?" Rapunzel continued. "Why did they cause my hair to grow back? Why did they chase us? Why—"

"Shh, Raps!" Cassandra whispered. She

glanced around, worried. "We can't tell anyone about that night."

Rapunzel lifted a lock of her long hair. "I think the secret is pretty much out, don't you?"

It had been impossible for Rapunzel to hide her newly long blond hair after they'd returned to the castle. There was too much of it!

She had finally confessed to her father about sneaking out, and had told him about the strange rocks. He forbade her to go beyond the walls of their kingdom again without his permission.

"We can't tell *anyone*," Cassandra repeated. "If your father finds out I helped you sneak out, he'll banish me from the kingdom!"

Cassandra had been adopted and raised by the captain of the royal guard, and she was as skilled in sword-fighting as she was in braiding hair. It was her dream to one day get rid of the silk dress and veiled headpiece she had to wear as a lady-in-waiting and join the Corona royal guard herself.

"Don't worry," Rapunzel assured her. "I told my father I snuck out alone." She didn't plan to tell *anyone* the whole truth.

Well, except for the one person she *had* to tell.

"I have to tell Eugene what happened, though," she said.

"No, you don't," Cassandra insisted, placing a flower in Rapunzel's hair and tugging the braid tight. "As far as he knows, you woke up one morning with blond hair. That's all he *needs* to know."

"But he's my boyfriend!" Rapunzel protested. "We tell each other everything."

Cassandra was only a few years older than Rapunzel, but because Rapunzel had spent so much of her life cut off from the world, she seemed younger. She could be too trusting, thought Cassandra, wanting to see only the good in people. Cassandra, on the other hand, knew that even good people had flaws.

She stepped in front of Rapunzel and took her hands. "*Please*, Raps," she said. "Don't tell Eugene."

"Tell Eugene what?" Eugene bounced into the room, a coy smile on his face. "Are you two keeping secrets from me?"

Rapunzel looked from Eugene to Cassandra, torn. "Um . . ."

"Come on, Blondie," Eugene said, meeting Rapunzel's green eyes with his warm brown ones. "It's me, Eugene. You can trust *me*."

Eugene had helped Rapunzel find the confidence to leave the tower. He'd defended her from Mother Gothel and given up his life as a thief to stay with her in the castle. Didn't those things *prove* he was trustworthy?

"*I* don't trust you," Cassandra said before Rapunzel could reply. "You have a big mouth."

Eugene glared at her, offended. "Name one time I blew a secret," he demanded.

"When you told Queen Arianna what Raps had given her for her birthday *before* the queen opened her present," Cassandra said. "When you told me about my surprise party a week early. When—"

"I said *one*," Eugene snapped. "That's two already."

"I could go on, if you want," Cassandra replied. "And on, and on, and on . . ."

Eugene ignored her and turned to Rapunzel. "You're *really* not going to tell me?"

Rapunzel hated being caught between Eugene and Cassandra, two of her favorite people in the world. She trusted both of them with her life.

But with secrets . . . ?

"I'm sorry," Rapunzel said to Eugene.

"Fine," Eugene said. Rapunzel could see the

hurt in his eyes. "There are plenty of *other* people who trust me with their secrets—and I'm going to find some now." He marched out before Rapunzel could stop him.

Rapunzel turned to Cassandra. "Maybe we're being unfair to him," she said.

Cassandra shook her head. "Listen, we may be able to get some answers about your hair *ourselves.* Just the two of us."

"How?" Rapunzel asked.

"I know someone who might help. His name is Varian, and he's some kind of wizard."

Rapunzel perked up. "A real wizard?" She had never seen a wizard, but she'd read about them in books. "Do you think he'll have one of those pointy hats?" she asked, remembering the illustrations she'd seen. "And a robe and a staff? And cast spells and—"

"No, I don't." Cassandra grabbed Rapunzel's arms and looked her in the eyes, serious. "Very little is known about Varian, Raps. And what *is* known isn't good. Some say he's dangerous. Possibly even *deadly*."

Rapunzel thought it over. "But if we want answers, he's our best bet, right?"

Cassandra nodded.

"Well then," Rapunzel told her. "It looks like we've got a wizard to visit."

A few miles from the castle, at the edge of the forest, sat the Snuggly Duckling tavern. Eugene had spent a lot of time there when he was a thief and known by his alias, Flynn Rider.

"There they are!" Eugene called out to the patrons as he entered the tavern with Maximus, a horse and an official member of the royal guard. While Eugene and Max had once been enemies, they had bonded over their shared love for Rapunzel.

The pub was filled with the usual collection of thugs and hooligans. *My pals,* thought Eugene.

Guys who would gladly share their secrets with me. There was an old saying: "Honor among thieves." This meant that Eugene would surely find *someone* inside the tavern who trusted him.

He waited, but none of the men spoke up. "Come on! Doesn't *anyone* want to share anything with me? No secrets, no news—"

"I've got news," Hook Foot growled from under his seat. "You can't keep a secret."

Eugene frowned. He couldn't believe even *criminals* refused to trust him.

Just then, Big Nose entered the tavern holding a bouquet of flowers.

"Big Nose!" Eugene said to his friend. "Are those for your girlfriend? How are you two doing?"

"Glad you asked!" Big Nose replied. Eugene

smiled, pleased that Big Nose was willing to share something personal with him. "Perhaps this latest poem I wrote will answer your question."

The other thugs groaned.

After meeting Rapunzel, who had en-couraged the thugs to follow their dreams, Big Nose had become a poet. But his poems could be epic—which means very, *very* long.

Big Nose unfolded a piece of paper. "It's called 'Can You Keep a Secret? I Love You,'" he said. He cleared his throat and began to read. "'Our love is like a timeless truth. It knows no tick nor tock. Our love is a big toe of honesty, poking through a hole in your favorite sock. . . .'"

Eugene could feel the other thugs glaring at him as Big Nose went on . . . and on and on. Max, bored, *clip-clop*ped over to the window.

Eugene clapped, interrupting Big Nose. "Great poem! Thanks for sharing!"

"Sharing is what the poem's about!" Big Nose responded with a smile. "Because if you can't share everything with someone special, maybe that someone *isn't* so special."

These words struck Eugene hard. Did Rapunzel's refusal to trust him mean maybe he wasn't so special to *her*?

Eugene felt a tug on his collar as Max dragged him to the tavern window. Outside, they could see Rapunzel and Cassandra on another palace horse, Fidella, riding into the forest.

"Where are they going?" Eugene said to himself. It was another secret Rapunzel was keeping from him.

He decided to follow them. Whatever was going on . . . it wouldn't be a secret for long.

"So this is where Varian lives?" Rapunzel asked as she and Cassandra climbed down from Fidella. Pascal perched on her shoulder.

In front of them was a house. It sat atop a set of wide stone stairs and was tall and narrow.

"It seems cozy . . . ," Rapunzel continued. "In an 'I wish

I'd said goodbye to my loved ones before I left' kind of way."

Cassandra tied Fidella to a post near an apple tree. She and Rapunzel each took in a brave breath and headed up the stairs to the house's entrance.

They entered together, stepping into a dark hallway. Ahead, eerie green light seeped around the edges of a closed door. Cassandra carefully pushed the door open, revealing a room filled with fog.

Rapunzel followed Cassandra inside. Neither of them saw the string stretching across the floor. Cassandra stepped on it, triggering a bottle of bubbling liquid on a shelf above them to tip over. The liquid oozed onto the floor.

POOF! Their feet were suddenly trapped in a sticky, bubble-gum-like goo.

A moment later, a hulking figure emerged from the fog. Red eyes glowed from the mask the figure wore over its face. "WHAT DO YOU WANT?" the figure boomed.

"We're, um, looking for Varian," Rapunzel said, her voice shaking. Pascal, clinging to her, hunched in fear.

"I . . . AM . . . VARIAN!"

He was unlike any wizard Rapunzel had seen in books. She swallowed her fear and gave him her friendliest smile. "Sorry to bother you, sir," she said. "We wanted to ask you about my hair, since you're a magic expert—"

"*MAGIC?*" Varian yelled. "I do not work with *magic!*" He lifted off his mask—revealing a short fourteen-year-old boy with shaggy brown hair, freckles, and a goofy grin.

Cassandra and Rapunzel stared in shock.

Varian wasn't a scary wizard; he was just a kid.

Varian leaped down from a stool to the floor. "I mean, *technically*, it isn't magic. It's *alchemy*."

Rapunzel knew that word. Alchemy was like chemistry. Alchemists were scientists who examined liquids, powders, and other substances to see what they were made of. They also mixed those things together to make new substances—like the goo trapping the girls' feet.

"You've just stepped in one of my latest creations," Varian said proudly. "See, we have a bit of a critter problem here." He waved to a raccoon stuck in the goo near Rapunzel and Cassandra. "I whipped up this mixture to trap the little guys without hurting them."

"Riveting," Cassandra said. "But could you get us *out* of here, please?"

32

"Oh, right." Varian searched his lab coat pockets. "Where did I put that neutralizing powder . . . ?" Finally, he pulled out what looked like a saltshaker and sprinkled some powder over their feet.

The sticky goo disappeared and the girls were freed. The raccoon darted off.

"Sorry about that, Your Highness," Varian said to Rapunzel.

Rapunzel stared at him in surprise. "You know who I am?"

"How could I not? I mean, look at your *hair*!" Varian gestured to the long golden braid hanging down Rapunzel's back.

"Please," she said. "Call me Rapunzel."

"Really?" Varian was amazed that he could call a princess by her first name. "Wow, okay. Anyway, everyone in the kingdom's heard

about your long hair coming back." He leaned down and whispered. "People say it's magic, but I don't believe it. As a man of science—"

"That's why we're here," Cassandra said, interrupting him. "Listen, kid, we need your help to figure out what the deal is with her hair, and what might explain why it came back." She stepped closer to Varian and stared down at him. "But whatever we find out, you've got to keep it a secret. You can't tell *anyone*."

Varian gulped. He could tell Cassandra was serious. He nodded.

Varian had Rapunzel lie down on a lab table. She'd unbraided her hair, and it streamed out from the top of her head to the end of the table and down to the floor.

He peered at Rapunzel's hair through a magnifying glass attached to a long metal rod. Varian pressed his lips together as he studied the blond strands. "It's very . . . long," he said finally.

Cassandra rolled her eyes.

"But don't worry," he continued. "I'm sure I can unlock the mystery of

your hair with the power of science!" Varian threw his arms wide, hitting the rod holding the magnifying glass. The rod spun around and the glass smacked into the back of his head. "Ow!"

"Are you okay?" asked Rapunzel.

Varian patted his head with his hand. "Don't worry," he said. "It's just a little . . ."

He saw the blood on his hand. Suddenly, his eyes rolled back in his head and he collapsed to the floor.

Outside Varian's house, Eugene stood next to Max and Fidella at the apple tree. He'd been waiting for Rapunzel and Cassandra to come out for over an hour.

At first, Eugene had just been curious about what the girls were up to. Now he was getting worried. He no longer cared whether Rapunzel was keeping secrets from him. He just wanted her to be okay.

"I'm going in," he told the horses.

* * *

Back inside the house, Varian sat across from Rapunzel. Part of her hair was wrapped around his head, covering the wound.

Cassandra stood nearby and watched as Rapunzel, with Pascal on her lap, sang the song Mother Gothel had taught her.

"Bring back what once was mine," Rapunzel sang. The song had always caused her blond hair to glow and bring out its magical powers. She'd used that power to heal Eugene once, when he had cut his hand.

But her hair didn't glow this time. When Varian unwrapped it, the wound on his head was still there. "We've learned *one* thing about your hair," he said. "It no longer contains its legendary healing power." He smiled. "Progress!"

He leaped up and cracked his knuckles.

Varian's excitement at having a problem to solve made him forget his injury. "Now let's figure out exactly what that hair is made of!"

CHAPTER 4

"Are you *sure* about this, Raps?" Cassandra asked.

Rapunzel, strapped to another lab table, gave her a thumbs-up. "Let's do this!" She was eager to see a real alchemist-wizard at work.

The table was connected to a larger machine and had been tilted up so it was perpendicular to the floor. Several odd-looking gizmos with sharp teeth, clawlike hooks, and pointed edges hung above Rapunzel's head. Pascal sat protectively on her shoulder.

"This machine can analyze any substance and determine its exact chemical makeup," Varian explained. He was now wearing gloves and a pair of goggles, in addition to his lab coat. "It should tell us all we need to know about your hair."

Wires led from the table to a control panel covered with gears and dials. Above the dials was a pair of levers, which Varian grabbed with both hands and pulled.

Suddenly, the table spun upside down, taking Rapunzel with it. "Whoa!" she cried.

Pascal leaped off Rapunzel's shoulder as the table continued to swing around. While Rapunzel rotated, the clawlike gizmos grabbed chunks of her hair, tugging it and stretching it every which way. Cassandra watched, worried.

Varian yanked the levers up and the machine stopped. "Done!" he announced.

"Okay, not super-fun . . . ," Rapunzel said, breathless. "But at least it's over."

"I meant done with the first test," Varian said. "Only eighty-six more to go!"

Behind him, a bell rang on a cuckoo clock–shaped counter atop a tall pole. Numbers on the front of the counter clicked down from eighty-seven to eighty-six.

The lab table slammed down and Rapunzel was once again parallel to the floor. A round saw lowered toward her hair, which now streamed out from the top of her head. Rapunzel's eyes

43

went wide as she realized the saw was going to cut through her hair.

Except it didn't.

Instead, it clanged against the blond strands and broke off from its arm, flying toward Varian—who ducked just in time.

"Amazing!" Varian shouted, delighted. "Your hair's absolutely unbreakable!"

"I'm betting *you're* not!" Eugene burst through the laboratory door. "Let her go!" he told Varian.

"Eugene!" Rapunzel cried. The machine had flipped her upright again, and its gizmos were tugging and twisting her hair. The counter clanged and clicked down with each new test.

Eugene was stunned to see Rapunzel smiling. "Blondie! You're okay."

"Hey!" Varian exclaimed. "You're Flynn

Rider!" He clapped his gloved hands together, thrilled.

Eugene's thief instincts went on alert. His first thought was *Deny everything.* "I don't know what you're talking about," he told Varian.

Varian dashed to a wall and drew back a curtain to reveal a Wanted poster of Flynn

Rider, surrounded by shelves filled with Flynn Rider adventure books.

They were the same books Eugene had read when he was young. He'd taken the name Flynn Rider from the books' hero, since his real name, Eugene Fitzherbert, wasn't very impressive for a thief.

The face on the Wanted poster was really him. The daring adventurer in the books wasn't.

"You're my hero!" Varian told Eugene. "I've read every single book about you." He held up one of the books. "Remember the time you dueled that evil knight blindfolded?"

"Well, see, kid," Eugene said, "that wasn't actually *me*."

Varian grabbed a cattle-prod-like device and waved it around like a sword. "How about when you fought the Earl of Camembert?"

Eugene held up his arms protectively. "Would someone please explain to me who this child is?"

"I'm Varian, master alchemist!" Varian declared. Suddenly, the ground rumbled beneath them.

"What was that trembling?" Eugene asked.

"Trembling? I didn't notice any trembling," Varian said, quickly changing the subject. "I just remembered I need my spectro-metric press to read the results of the tests." He leaned in toward Eugene and whispered, "If you come with me, Flynn Rider, I'll show you something special. But you've *got* to keep it a secret."

"Me?" Eugene asked. "You want to tell *me* a secret?"

Varian nodded.

Eugene grinned. "Let's go!" he said.

Varian left Cassandra to keep watch over Rapunzel and the hair-testing machine. Then he led Eugene around the outside of his house, to a shed cluttered with tools and machine parts.

Varian sifted through the mess. "Got it!" he said, lifting up what looked like a typewriter with wires hanging from the bottom.

Suddenly, the earth shook again.

"Why does that keep happening?" Eugene asked worriedly.

Varian set down the press and pulled up a

49

trapdoor in the floor of the shed. "Flynn Rider," he said, his voice low and important. "I believe I promised you . . . a *secret*."

He grabbed a lantern and climbed down the ladder inside the trapdoor, disappearing into the darkness below. Eugene reluctantly followed him to an underground pathway beneath the floor.

"These tunnels run through my entire village," Varian told him. "Which makes them perfect for my project."

"What project?" Eugene asked, although he was afraid to hear the answer.

"This project!"

At the end of the pathway, Varian held up his lantern, revealing a huge tank as big as his house. Pipes sprouted from the sides and top like tentacles. A smaller machine, with

dials and levers, was attached to one side of the tank. Clouds of steam puffed and swirled around the contraption.

Varian pointed to a vat of chemicals sitting near the tank. "Through the miracle of alchemy, I found a way to heat this entire tank of water with a single drop of my newest, yet-to-be-named compound." His eyes brightened. "I'll call it Flynnoleum!"

Eugene looked at the tank, confused. "I don't get it," he said.

"I'm going to surprise my village by bringing the people hot running water!" Varian explained. "I built a system of pipes that run—"

The tank shuddered, causing the ground to shake.

"Those tremors," Eugene said. "Is it your machines that are causing them?"

"My *machines* aren't causing them. The chemical reactions they *trigger* are," said Varian.

"Listen, kid," Eugene said. "Anything that causes earthquakes can't be safe. We've got to warn people about this."

"You promised you'd keep it a secret!" cried Varian. "Besides, I'm an expert. It's all perfectly safe. I've adjusted my calculations for every possible outcome. The margin of error is less than point five-six percent . . . or was it point five-seven?"

Suddenly, a bolt popped off the side of the tank and whizzed past Eugene. It pierced the tunnel wall, inches from his terrified face.

Eugene looked over at Varian.

Varian shrugged sheepishly. "I suppose I could turn it down a *little*."

While Varian stayed behind to recalibrate his hot-water tank, Eugene carried the spectro-metric press back to the laboratory.

The hair-testing machine was still spinning Rapunzel around while pulling her hair in every direction—and she was still enjoying it. "Only s-s-seven m-more t-tests t-to g-go!" she declared as the machine jolted her back and forth.

Eugene plugged the press into the control panel the way Varian had told him. As he did, there was another tremor.

"It's time to go," he told Rapunzel. "*Now.* Somewhere far, far away."

The numbers flipped from "07" to "06" as the counter clanged.

"We can't leave," Rapunzel protested. "We're almost finished!"

Cassandra looked at Eugene suspiciously. "Why do you want us to leave so bad?"

"Because when that thing blows—" Eugene caught himself. He was determined to keep Varian's secret. "Never mind."

"When *what* thing blows?" Cassandra demanded.

The counter clicked down to "05." *CLANG!*

Eugene glanced out the window. The ground was shaking all around them.

The counter clicked to "04," then "03."

"Okay, okay!" Eugene threw up his hands.

"I wanted to prove I could keep a secret, but I can't! Varian has—"

The floor shook again, the biggest tremor yet. Eugene and Cassandra were thrown off-balance. The pole holding the counter tilted and Pascal jumped to the floor as the numbers clicked to "02."

"Varian built this huge tank and some sort of heater underground," Eugene went on. "Both machines are clearly unstable. They could blow up *any minute.*"

BOOM! A loud explosion rattled the walls.

"And that minute is *now,*" Eugene said.

Another *clang*—the counter flipped to "01."

Outside the window, chunks

of earth, gears, and machinery exploded from the ground and blasted into the sky.

"Get me out of this machine!" screamed Rapunzel.

Cassandra grabbed a wrench and banged at the contraption while Eugene tugged on Rapunzel's straps.

Varian ran past the window, still trying to fix things. "He's going to get himself killed," Eugene said.

"Get Rapunzel out of here!" Cassandra yelled to Eugene over the noise of the earthquake. "I'll get the kid!" She dashed out of the lab as Eugene struggled to free Rapunzel. The walls cracked around them. Chunks of the ceiling began to fall.

The counter flipped to "00." Just as the spectro-metric press started to spit out the results, a piece of the ceiling fell on the machine, crushing it. But Rapunzel was still trapped.

"You have to get out of here!" she told Eugene.

"No way," Eugene said, wrapping his arms around her. "I'm not going anywhere without you."

There was another rumble, and then another explosion. Eugene hugged Rapunzel tight. Pascal scurried under a blanket of Rapunzel's hair.

They all closed their eyes as the walls and ceiling collapsed on them.

Rapunzel could sense a warm light around

her and see a faint glow through her closed eyes. She waited for the rocks to crush them— but she didn't feel *anything*.

Suddenly, there was a burst of rocks exploding upward, followed by a clattering as the rubble fell to the ground.

Rapunzel slowly opened her eyes.

They were alive! Her hair had blossomed out around them like a giant canopy.

Eugene opened his eyes and looked up— and then at Rapunzel. "Did your hair . . . protect us?"

Rapunzel didn't have to say anything. She and Eugene both knew the answer was yes.

Cassandra and Varian were alive as well.

The explosions had propelled Varian's vat of Flynnoleum into the air, emptying its contents. As it flipped over and sped down toward him, Cassandra had run up to Varian and shielded him.

The open end of the vat had clamped down over them. Now they climbed out, shaken but unhurt.

Varian looked at Cassandra with awe. She had saved his life! "Thank you, milady," he said, gazing at her adoringly.

Cassandra rolled her eyes. Just what she needed—a would-be wizard with a crush on her.

"Varian!" a deep voice called out. A tall, broad-shouldered man ran toward them. It was Varian's father, Quirin. "Are you okay? What happened?" he asked. Quirin noticed

Varian's guilty expression. "Another one of your inventions?" he asked, gesturing to the rubble surrounding them.

"Sorry, Dad," Varian murmured.

Quirin frowned, disappointed. He turned away from his son and asked the assembled crowd if they were all right.

Cassandra left Varian with his father and ran off to check on Rapunzel. She was relieved to find the princess unharmed. Rapunzel explained how her hair had formed a magical shield to protect her, Eugene, and Pascal from the crumbling laboratory.

The girls agreed that the visit to Varian hadn't solved the mystery of Rapunzel's newly long blond hair. It had only raised more questions.

Thankfully, Max and Fidella were also

unharmed and they now stood by, ready to return everyone home.

But first, Rapunzel wanted to apologize to Eugene. "I'm so sorry," she told him. "From now on, no more secrets." She took a deep breath, ready to tell Eugene the truth—the *whole* truth. "You know how I said I just woke up with my hair long? I didn't. The night before that, Cass helped me break out of Corona."

"I knew it!" Eugene said. "She's going to get in *so* much trouble. . . ." Rapunzel gave him a warning look. "If anyone were to find out, that is," he added. "Which they won't. Because *this guy* can keep a secret." He pointed to his chest.

Rapunzel told him about going to the cliff where the golden flower had been found.

64

"There were these black rocks, and I know it sounds weird, but I think they're what made my hair grow back."

"After today, Rapunzel," Eugene said, "*nothing* sounds weird."

The End

CHAPTER 1

Cassandra stood on a ladder in the castle courtyard, struggling to tie a giant banner between two poles. The banner read EXPOSITION OF THE SCIENCES.

"I don't see why the lady-in-waiting has to help set up for this thing," she grumbled to herself. "Who'd even come to a dumb science expo? Dorks, that's who."

"Who's ready for the expo?" an excited voice cried out from below. "Woo-hoo!"

Cassandra looked down to see Varian enter the courtyard pushing a cart. He was dressed in his usual scientist getup: lab coat, rubber gloves, and a pair of goggles around his neck.

Cassandra and Rapunzel had met Varian when they'd visited him for help in figuring out why Rapunzel's long blond hair had grown back. Cassandra had heard Varian was a wise old wizard, but he turned out to be a teenage alchemist who liked to invent strange things— like the hot-water tank that had nearly blown them all up.

"Hey, Cassie," Varian said. "Want to see my new invention? It's a special device that can create an entirely new element, which I've named—"

"First off, it's Cass or Cassandra, not Cassie," Cassandra said. She knew Varian had had a crush on her ever since she'd saved his life in the explosion at his house. A lovelorn alchemist was the last thing she needed in her life right now. "Second, I'm seriously behind on my chores, so—"

"Cassandra!" A castle guard named Stan ran toward her. "I thought you should know that the captain is short on guards for the expo today."

Cassandra scrambled down the ladder. Her father was the captain of the guard and had adopted her as a baby. He'd taught her all about fighting and defending the kingdom. It was her dream to become a member of the royal guard herself. Today could be her chance!

Cassandra leaped off the bottom rung of the ladder and grabbed Stan's arm. "Let's go!" she cried.

Varian watched her leave, disappointed.

"Hey, Cassandra! Looking good!" a voice called.

Varian turned to find Rapunzel staring at him through eyeglasses that looked like a pair of short telescopes.

"You should see some of the inventions on display," she said. "Look at these crazy goggles." Her magnified eyes squinted at Varian as she leaned closer. "Oh, hi, Varian! Sorry, I thought you were Cass." Rapunzel took off the glasses. "It's nice to see you!"

Varian's good mood returned. "I wouldn't have missed this expo for anything!" he said. "Wait until you see my invention!"

"Is this one deadly, too?" asked Eugene, who had arrived behind Rapunzel. Eugene had been at Varian's house with Rapunzel and Cassandra when the hot-water tank had exploded.

"Ha, ha. No," Varian said. "I think you and everyone else at the expo will be *quite* impressed. Including Cassandra." He looked at Rapunzel with a hopeful expression. "She'll be there, right?"

"Of course," said Rapunzel. "I'm sure she doesn't have anything going on that is more important than *this*."

Stan and Cassandra hurried down the hall toward the captain's quarters. Cassandra hadn't had time to change out of her lady-in-waiting dress and into the tunic, tights, and boots she normally wore for guard training. This would have to do.

Stan opened the door and Cassandra snuck in just as her dad shouted, "We need more guards!" He was busy working out plans to patrol the big science expo. When he caught sight of his daughter, he asked the nearby guards to leave the room.

"So, you want your first guard assignment?" he said to her. Cassandra nodded. The captain shook his head. "I just don't know whether you're ready."

"I've been training since I was six," Cassandra protested. "I know all the rules of guarding better than anyone. So if there's any reason why you feel I'm not ready—*besides* my being your daughter—I'm all ears."

The captain thought it over. He *did* need more guards for the expo. "Very well. But your lady-in-waiting duties come first. Only when you finish those may you help. Are we clear?"

Cassandra was thrilled. That was good enough for her. "Crystal clear!" she said.

* * *

A corner of the courtyard had been blocked off as a reception area for the inventors and important guests to gather after the expo. It was Cassandra's job to set out flowers, juice, and pastries on the reception tables.

"There you are!" Varian called to her. "We didn't finish our conversation earlier! I was telling you about my invention. I really think you'll love it, but it takes two people to operate it. So how about being my assistant?"

Cassandra spun around to face him. "Assistant? No—*ah! No!*"

This last "no" wasn't to Varian. When she'd spun around, Cassandra had knocked over a pitcher of juice. A purple stain spread across the white tablecloth. "Noooo," she groaned.

"Allow me," said Varian. He took a tube of white crystals from his pocket and shook a few onto the stain. Then he added water from a vase and the crystals exploded, sending out a purplish mist. The mist cleared . . . and the stain was gone!

"How did you do that?" asked Cassandra.

Varian held up the tube. "Rock salt. It mixed with the water from the flowers and the acid from the grape juice and absorbed the stain." He grinned. "Alchemy!"

Cassandra studied him, sensing that his science skills might come in handy with her chores. "Any chance you'd want to—"

"Help you? I'd love to!" Varian said. "And

then you can help me—and be my assistant! It'll only take a minute."

Cassandra thought it over. If she could get through her chores quickly, she'd save time, which meant she'd have at least a minute to spare to help out Varian.

"Deal," she told him.

As they went to work on her chores, Varian surprised Cassandra with his many useful inventions. He had a machine that polished eight spoons at once and a potion that could perk up droopy flowers in seconds.

His best invention, though, was a handful of blue marbles. He scattered them down a long castle hallway that would have taken Cassandra hours to mop. The marbles foamed up, covering the stones in frothy soap. Then he tossed a yellow marble into the suds and—*POOF!* The suds disappeared, leaving the floor sparkling clean.

Despite Varian's help, by the time the clock tower bell tolled twelve, Cassandra was still only halfway through her chores. "There's no way I'll finish before the expo," she moaned.

"Why don't I finish your chores for you?" Varian suggested. "Then you can start your guard duty and we'll meet up later—and you can help me with my demonstration."

"You'd do that?" Cassandra asked.

"No problem," Varian said. "It's what friends do, right?"

Were they friends? Varian *had* helped her. A lot. What could it hurt to say yes?

"Right," she said. "Friends."

Tents had been placed around Corona's town square for the kingdom's inventors to show off their ideas before the official demonstration. Rapunzel dragged Eugene from one tent to the next, amazed by the objects on display. Eugene had brought popcorn along to munch on.

They stopped at one tent where a woman sat on a stool with pedals attached. The pedals were connected by a rod to a pitcher. When the woman pressed down on the pedals, the pitcher poured batter onto a griddle atop a small cast-iron stove. The batter sizzled, and a few seconds later, a mechanical spatula flipped the flapjack to cook the other side.

"Wow!" declared Rapunzel. "That makes flipping flapjacks look like a piece of cake!" She grinned at Eugene. "Or should I say a *pancake*?" She giggled. Eugene smiled.

In the next tent, a farmer stood beside a wooden pen with two hoses running out from under it. One hose was attached to a pump, which the farmer pressed with his foot. This caused the hose to milk the goat inside the pen. The milk dripped through the other hose into a large pail. Suddenly, a head popped out from inside the milk pail.

"Shorty!" Eugene called out. Shorty was one of the pub thugs from the Snuggly Duckling, a tavern where Eugene had hung out back when he was a thief. Shorty was the shortest and oldest of the thugs, and he tended to fall asleep in the oddest places.

Shorty sat in the milk and slurped it up through a straw. "Mmmm!" he declared.

Eugene spit out his popcorn, his appetite gone.

KAPOW! Colorful smoke exploded from the tent next door. Eugene and Rapunzel forgot about Shorty and the spoiled milk as a tall, pretty woman emerged from the smoke.

"Attention, science lovers!" the woman shouted. "I am the one, the only, Fernanda Pizzazzo!" She waved to a table covered with a velvet tarp. "What stupendimonious invention lies beneath this veil, you ask? You'll find out when master scientist Dr. Alcott St. Croix arrives to give *my* invention first prize!"

Rapunzel was wowed. The inventors were all so creative! She herself had painted pictures and built mobiles and baked cakes—but those were things that already existed. She had never made anything *new* like the things she had seen today.

Rapunzel turned to Eugene, her eyes bright with excitement. "I'm going to invent something, too," she declared, and ran off.

It didn't take Rapunzel long to come up with something to show Eugene. She remembered she'd *already* invented something, when she lived in the tower: a way to play catch by herself. She invited Eugene to her art studio to see it.

"I give you . . . the Hey-Hey!" Rapunzel announced, lifting a small wooden spool with a long piece of string wrapped around it. She held the end of the string and threw the spool in front of her. The spool flew out as the string unwound, then returned to her hand as it rewound in the other direction.

"It *is* amazing, Blondie," Eugene told her. "But it's already been invented. It's called a yo-yo."

Rapunzel let the spool fall, disappointed. But she wasn't about to give up. "Luckily, I have another idea," she said, leading him across the room to a table covered with plates of vegetables.

"Carrots, celery, cucumbers," she said. "What do these foods have in common?"

"I don't eat them?" Eugene deadpanned. He was more of a popcorn and pretzels kind of guy.

"No! We chop them!" said Rapunzel. "But knives can be dangerous. That's why I invented . . ." She reached behind the table and lifted up what looked like a miniature guillotine. "The Safety Slicer!"

Eugene gulped. Regular-sized guillotines were used to chop the heads off criminals. Even though Rapunzel had painted the slicer pink and decorated it with flowers, the blade was still scarily sharp.

Rapunzel placed a carrot inside the hole under the blade while Pascal supervised from nearby. "Load it up and . . ." She dropped the blade, which cut neatly through the top of the carrot.

Eugene put his hand on his neck.

"It seems a little . . . extreme. Besides, I think they have something like that already, too."

Rapunzel frowned. It wasn't fair. She'd been locked in a tower for eighteen years! How could she possibly know everything that had ever been invented? Would she *ever* be able to come up with something new?

CHAPTER 3

Cassandra and Pete stood in the hallway Varian had cleaned with his magic marbles. Cassandra had been happy with how shiny he'd gotten it—but she hadn't wanted to stare at it all day.

Her father had put her on "backup duty." That meant she had to stand at attention inside the castle and wait. She wouldn't be given any special duties unless she needed to replace another guard.

Even worse, she was *second* backup to Pete,

the first backup. At least she got to wear the official guard uniform.

Just then, the captain of the guard appeared at the end of the hallway with Stan. "You'll be Dr. St. Croix's personal guard," the captain told him. "It's probably the most important job of the day." Dr. St. Croix had been invited to the expo to judge the inventions.

"Thank you, Captain," said Stan. "I'm honored to—*ah!*" Stan's feet shot out in front of him and he crashed to the floor. "Ow!"

Cassandra spotted the puddle Stan had slipped in. It seemed Varian's marbles hadn't *completely* dried the floor.

The captain frowned and waved Pete over. "You'll need to replace Stan."

Pete, thrilled, dashed toward the captain. "Right away, Cap—*ah!*" Pete's foot hit the same

At the far end of the room was a raised platform covered by a velvet curtain.

"Behind that curtain lies the royal seal of Equis," the king told Eugene, yanking the curtain aside.

Eugene stared. He was shocked, stunned, bewildered . . . and speechless.

Sitting atop the platform was a seal. Not the silver or brass kind, with the image of the kingdom stamped on it. This was a *seal*. A live, whiskered, blubbery sea mammal–type seal. The kind that lived in the ocean—or *should*, anyway.

"Arf!" barked the seal.

CHAPTER 4

"It's a seal," Eugene said, once his power of speech had returned.

"Indeed," the king declared. "The royal seal!"

"It's a *seal* seal," protested Eugene. "Not a royal seal."

"It's a *seal* seal owned by a king," the king explained. "And thus a royal seal."

Eugene considered pointing out how ridiculous it was for King Trevor to have a marine creature as a "royal seal," but it wasn't worth the time. They needed to get out of the castle with the animal before they were caught. "Just grab one end and let's go," he told the king.

Instead, King Frederic crossed the room to a portrait of King Trevor on the wall. He took a paintbrush from his satchel. "What should I paint?" he asked Eugene. "An eye patch? Some stink lines? A tear representing Trevor's embarrassment when he realizes I've outpranked him?"

"None of those things!" cried Eugene. "We've got to go—*now!*" He threw out his arms in frustration, accidentally slapping the seal. The creature let out a loud "ARF!" in response.

A second later, footsteps sounded from the hallway.

Eugene looked around for an escape. He glanced at the ceiling and got an idea. "I'm going to need your rope," he told the king.

When the guards stormed in a few seconds later, Eugene, the king, and the seal were gone.

Or at least, they *seemed* to be gone. They were actually hiding in the chandelier, which dangled over the guards' heads.

As the guards searched the room, King Frederic whispered to Eugene, "What're we going to do?"

Eugene stared at the king in disbelief. "*Now you want my advice?*"

"You're the expert," said the king.

"That's what I tried to tell you from the start!"

As they argued, the chandelier swayed. The bolts connecting it to the ceiling twisted loose and fell to the floor one by one. Suddenly, the chandelier broke free—crashing to the ground!

The guards surrounded Eugene and the king, spears pointed at the two burglars.

"Arf!" barked the seal.

"Well," said the king. "It seems this prank has gone horribly wrong."

King Frederic slumped sadly next to Eugene inside a dark dungeon cell. Eugene felt sorry for him. Eugene himself had made lots of mistakes during his time as a thief, and he knew how bad it felt. But he imagined it must feel much worse to be a *king* and mess up.

"I'm sorry I lost my temper," he told the king. "It's just that this was my chance to get you to take me seriously for once."

King Frederic stared at Eugene, surprised. He hadn't thought much about Eugene's feelings during this whole adventure. He'd been too focused on embarrassing Trevor.

"You brought my daughter home to me after eighteen long years," the king told him. "If there's one man in the whole world I take *very* seriously, it's you."

Eugene was amazed. King Frederic didn't think he was just some nitwit thief—he actually had respect for him!

"Thanks, Your Majesty," he said. "May I ask then why you *didn't* listen to my ideas when we were breaking into the castle?"

The king sighed. "Sometimes I let good ideas slip through the cracks. I should have given your plan a chance."

"What you *should* have done was stayed in your own kingdom, Frederic," a voice called.

Eugene and King Frederic looked up to see King Trevor standing in the dungeon hallway, holding the seal tightly on a leash. The seal stared at Eugene and King Frederic with a sad expression and tears in its eyes.

King Trevor sneered at the prisoners. "Your efforts to steal Trevor, Jr., were comical at best."

"Your seal doesn't look too happy," Eugene observed.

King Frederic stood and faced King Trevor

through the bars of the cell. "All right, Trevor. You've had your laughs," he said. "Now release us."

"I'll let you go," replied King Trevor. "But not until I parade you through town wearing nothing but a jester's hat—proving once again that Equis is superior to Corona! Until then, I'm leaving you here to stew in the stench of your own defeat!"

King Trevor cackled as he yanked on the seal's leash, dragging the poor animal after him.

King Frederic plopped onto the cot and sighed. "Trevor's right," he said.

"You don't smell that bad, Your Majesty," Eugene assured him. "Besides, the stench in here is mostly from the seal. It's all that fish they eat."

"I *meant* I deserve to wear nothing but a jester's hat," said the king. "Once again, Trevor has proven he's the better prankster."

"*Better?*" replied Eugene. "His prank with your statue wasn't even funny! I mean, I laughed a *little*. But still. On the whole? Not that funny."

The king nodded. "True. His pranks are always more grating than humorous."

"Grating . . . ," Eugene murmured to himself.

"It means 'annoying' or 'irritating' or—"

"No, no," Eugene said. "*Grating*—that's how we get out of here!" He pointed to a grate in the floor of the cell. "The question is, are you willing to try it *my* way this time?"

CHAPTER 5

"Your Majesty! There's no way you'll escape *that* way!"

The two guards posted outside the dungeon door heard Eugene call out. They rushed into the dungeon and dashed to the cell to find Eugene alone.

"The king escaped without me!" Eugene told the guards, pointing to the floor of the cell. The grate was gone.

The guards hurriedly unlocked the cell door to investigate. They leaned down and peered into the hole in the floor.

"Lose something?" called a voice.

The guards glanced around, confused. The voice hadn't come from below. They looked up just as King Frederic, who had been hiding in the rafters, jumped on top of them, knocking them to the ground.

Eugene helped the king up off the dazed guards. "Well played, Your Majesty," he said with a smile. "Well played."

Back at the castle of Corona, things were also looking up for Maximus, a horse in the royal guard. Max was drinking from his trough when he spotted an apple on the ground nearby. It had appeared out of nowhere—as if by magic! Apples were Max's favorite.

He didn't notice the string attached to it and was about to

bite down on the apple when it darted out of his reach. Max followed the apple as it rolled toward the open doors of the stable barn.

Inside the barn, the apple came to a stop near a pile of hay. At last! Max opened his mouth wide . . . and bit into nothing. The string had yanked the apple into the shadows.

The barn doors crashed closed behind him. Max looked around nervously as footsteps thundered above him.

Suddenly, Rapunzel jumped from the rafters to the hay-strewn ground. "Gotcha!" she cried.

Max watched, confused, as Rapunzel dashed around the barn, yanking down the curtains covering the walls. When she was done, Max stared in shock.

Towers of apples lined the barn. In front of one wall stood a sculpture of a horse made entirely of apples. It was Max's dream come true!

Rapunzel laughed and pointed at him. "You should see the look on your face!"

Max galloped straight into the sculpture and bit an apple. It was delicious!

Rapunzel left Max in the barn to gobble up the apples. Outside, Cassandra leaned against a wall.

"Did you see the look on his face?" Rapunzel asked her. "He expected one apple, but he got a whole bunch!" She grinned. "Best. Prank. *Ever!* He was totally Rapunzeled!"

Cassandra nodded. "Unexpected, clever, and funny. But there's one more thing a great prank has to be. . . ."

Rapunzel frowned. What could be left?

Cassandra smiled. "A prank has to be *mischievous*, too," she said.

Eugene and King Frederic hadn't carried out a great prank, either. But that was about to change.

They had locked the two guards in the cell and taken their uniforms. The disguises had been Eugene's original plan to get them *inside* the castle without being caught. Now he hoped the disguises would get them *out*.

Unfortunately, as Eugene and the king headed toward the castle entrance, King Trevor appeared at the opposite end of the hall.

King Frederic turned to go back the way they'd come, but Eugene grabbed his arm.

"Wait," he whispered, recognizing the hall from when he'd broken in before. "Follow my lead. . . ."

Before the king could answer, Eugene dashed to a door and rattled the handle. The king followed. Eugene looked over at the king and winked just as King Trevor marched toward them, dragging Trevor, Jr., on his leash.

King Frederic was confused. Was it Eugene's plan to get caught? But the king decided to trust him this time, and he hurried to Eugene's side.

King Trevor arrived beside them. "It appears *someone* hasn't learned their lesson yet," he said.

Eugene threw his hands up in surrender. "You got us!"

King Frederic slowly raised his hands as well, although he wondered now if trusting Eugene had been a mistake. Playing along, he said, "We wanted to pull off *some* sort of prank so our trip wasn't completely in vain."

Eugene added, "I thought it'd be funny to break into the library and rearrange the newspapers. Historians hate that."

King Trevor rolled his eyes. "That is the worst idea for a prank I've ever heard! And once again, you'd have failed!" He pointed to the door across the hall. "*That* is the door to the library!"

Eugene shook his head. "I'm pretty sure *this* is the library," he said.

"You idiot! This is *my* castle!" exclaimed King Trevor. "I know where my own library is!" He pushed Eugene and King Frederic aside, threw open the door, and stepped inside—right onto a trapdoor.

The trapdoor snapped open and Trevor plummeted out of sight with a scream.

Eugene called down through the opening. "Forgot about your own top-notch security, did you?"

King Trevor yelled up from inside the trap. "Let me out, Frederic! There are spiders down here! *Ach!* One just touched me!"

King Frederic chuckled. He nodded to Eugene, impressed. "Well played, Eugene. Well played." The king raised his hand in the air, palm facing out. "Up high," he said.

Eugene hesitated, but this time the king kept his hand up. Eugene smiled and slapped King Frederic's hand.

The seal clapped his fins.

"Trevor, Jr., are you clapping?" King Trevor called. "Those better be claps of sorrow." The seal grinned and clapped harder.

King Frederic smiled at Eugene. "At last! I've finally humiliated Trevor."

"Oh, Your Majesty," Eugene said with a grin. "We have not yet *begun* to humiliate that guy."

All the way home to Corona, Eugene and King Frederic laughed, remembering how they'd tied King Trevor to the leg of his own statue in the Equis town square. They'd left him wearing nothing but a jester's hat—and a sign covering his body that read CORONA RULES!

The captain of the guard met Eugene and the king outside the Corona castle gates.

"Did you do it, Your Majesty?" the captain asked. "Did you get the seal?"

"We got him, Captain," the king replied. "But we let him go." He explained how they'd traveled to the seaside after leaving Equis and set Trevor, Jr., free.

"It's been an *excellent* day," the king declared as they neared the castle archway.

But then he saw it. . . .

The arch's gray stones had been painted pink and purple, and the whole structure was covered with pictures of daisies and birds.

"I guess we're not going with the lion theme," observed Eugene.

"I might have preferred it," replied the king.

Rapunzel popped out from behind the archway, a big grin on her face. "Gotcha, Dad!"

She laughed. "Oh man, you should *see* the look on your face!" The king chuckled. He was in a good mood from succeeding with his prank. It was only fair that he allow his daughter one of her own.

"I suppose it's fine," he told her. "As long as you and Cassandra repaint it—*today*."

Rapunzel held up two cans of gray paint. "Obviously, Dad," she said.

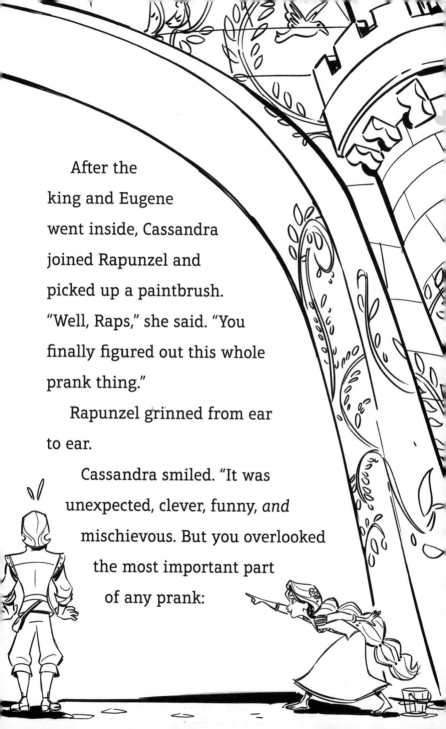

After the king and Eugene went inside, Cassandra joined Rapunzel and picked up a paintbrush. "Well, Raps," she said. "You finally figured out this whole prank thing."

Rapunzel grinned from ear to ear.

Cassandra smiled. "It was unexpected, clever, funny, *and* mischievous. But you overlooked the most important part of any prank:

You didn't think it through." She tossed a paintbrush to Rapunzel. "Now we have to repaint this whole thing by tonight."

Rapunzel handed the brush back to Cassandra. "Sorry, but I've got princess duties. Looks like you'll have to repaint it by yourself. Still believe I didn't think it through?" She snickered and skipped off toward the castle.

Cassandra stared at the paintbrush in her hand, then up at the huge stone archway—which would take *hours* to repaint by herself.

She groaned.

"Kidding!" a voice called from behind her. "I'm going to help you!" It was Rapunzel. She pointed a finger at Cassandra. "I totally got you, Cass! You should have seen the look on your face!" Rapunzel laughed as she picked up her paintbrush.

Cassandra shook her head. "I've been Rapunzeled," she said. Rapunzel giggled.

Cassandra dipped her brush in the paint and went to work next to Rapunzel. "Well played, Raps," she said with a sly smile. "Well played."

The End

Find out what happens next by reading more
TALES OF RAPUNZEL
adventures!

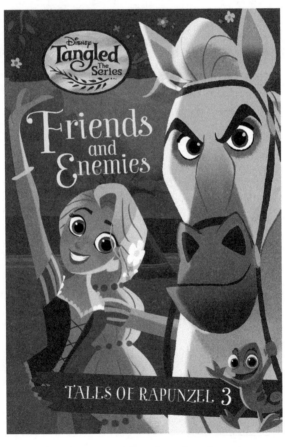

Don't miss book #3:
Friends and Enemies